Kingdom of Teeth

Michelle GARZA   Melissa LASON

The Sisters of Slaughter

ERASERHEAD PRESS
PORTLAND, OREGON

ERASERHEAD PRESS
P.O. BOX 10065
PORTLAND, OR 97296

www.eraserheadpress.com
facebook/eraserheadpress

ISBN: 978-1-62105-263-0
Copyright © 2018 by Michelle Garza and Melissa Lason
Cover art copyright © 2018 Erik Wilson

Printed in the USA.

For The Tooth Fairy

A Kingdom Corroded

"She's riddled with it," Dentin said. "Holes as big as a man's fist."

Queen Bicuspa lamented. "Her power will be lost forever."

They made their way to the sickroom bedside. The stink was palpable, twisting the guts, filling the heart with hopeless pity.

"And the children are doomed," Bicuspa added.

The invalid's head lolled on a pus-stained pillow as she fought to make eye contact with her two visitors.

She had once been a radiant, gleaming ivory, her flesh embedded with rows of white teeth. The last of the known Wisdoms in Molarous, the plague had taken hold of her and would be her end.

Black pits dotted her once pearly armor, revealing her soft, vulnerable insides. The Wisdoms felt everything around them much more strongly than the ordinary Hyperdontian; they were filled with nerve endings that connected to spirit world. Hers were now exposed to the dank castle air, setting them afire with suffering of herself and the people of the fair city beyond the window. What little skin showed between her adornment of molars, bicuspids and incisors was raised into festering yellow abscesses.

Pain filled her milky white eyes; her agony had to be incomprehensible. Even Hyperdontia's fairy queen was powerless to stop her oldest advisor from rotting away to nothing.

With an effort, the Wisdom spoke. "There is but one hope. A human. Only he can stop the nameless one."

At her words, they moved closer. The Wisdoms weren't gifted with the ability to see the future until their demise drew near; it was a terrible sign for her to speak of a hero.

"A human?" Dentin asked.

"His name is Plumber. Randy Plumber."

Bicuspa gazed past the deathbed to the open window. The Hyperdontians slept in fear, not knowing where the plague would strike next.

Her heart fluttered, her wings hung limp on her pale back. She wore her usual attire for the nights she collected teeth from the children of Earth: a close-fitting white dress tied at the waist with a shimmering ribbon. But, for the first time in the kingdom's short yet brutal war with the plague bringers, she felt the fire in her dying.

Dentin placed a hand on her shoulder and she turned to face him. She knew her countenance was gaunt, her usual wide, toothy grin drooping in a lipless frown.

His expression told her he still found her radiant, even in her darkest hour.

"We will find a way," he said. "The Wisdom has seen something."

She nodded. "Open the portal."

"And risk drawing the attention of the nameless one?" Dentin asked.

"We must."

"I won't even know where to locate this human."

"She will guide us, one last time," Bicuspa said, turning her attention to the figure that moaned and weakly shifted on the sheets of her bed.

"Make haste, child," the Wisdom said. She coughed until a mouthful of black sludge came rolling down her tooth-studded chin. From where he had been waiting in a discreet corner of the room, Dr. Maxillary hurried to her bedside.

"The exertion will surely kill her..." the doctor began, only to have the Wisdom raise a hand completely embedded with rotting teeth, their nerves exposed by the hungry plague. He fell silent.

"Open the portal, mother." Bicuspa spoke respectfully.

The Wisdom motioned in the air with one trembling finger, tracing the sacred sign. She then used the last of her strength to extract a tooth embedded at her wrist, an offering to the old gods.

A dim blue glow appeared. It grew from a pinpoint, larger and larger. She tossed the extracted tooth into the glow and a small rift opened and widened in its path.

"In my final moments," she said, her voice a powerful command for all its trembling hoarseness, "I seek the one revealed to me in my final dreams. The human, Plumber is his name."

The rift became a doorway, revealing an otherworldly scene. Without hesitation, Dentin stepped into it and passed through.

The queen held her breath and waited, wondering if the Wisdom had enough strength to hold the doorway open until he returned.

If not, he'd be doomed to stay in that foreign land until another Wisdom presented, or perish there a freak from another plane.

"I am dying," the Wisdom spoke, as if reading her worried queen's mind, "but there will be others like me. There always have been, and always will be. Wait for their guidance."

A Hero Known As Randy

Randy locked the office door and watched through the blinds as Jerry sped away in his sports car, blond hair fluttering gloriously, speakers blasting a power ballad from the eighties.

The car headed down Main Street toward the condo Jerry shared with Sherrie. For years, Randy had accused his brother of stealing her right out of his grasp ... only to have Jerry remind him he couldn't steal something that had never belonged to Randy to begin with.

Pangs of jealousy jabbed the pit of his stomach. How could brothers be so opposite? Here he was, pasty, pudgy and losing his hair, while his brother was a fair-haired Adonis of the dental community. His looks weren't the only thing he lacked in compared to Jerry. He'd never accomplished anything either. Randy was a disappointment, something his father never let him forget even until the day the old man died.

He made his way around the front desk and sighed at the stacks of paperwork his brother left behind for him, acting like it wasn't a big deal for Randy to spend an extra two hours in the office on a Friday. Randy had originally planned on heading down to Peckers for dinner and a drink. Tanya would be performing on the main stage, and Randy didn't want to miss those big saggy naturals. But he knew if he didn't finish logging in the new patient information, his brother would go ballistic.

If he had just finished school, he too could be a hotshot dentist and not the secretary and janitor of their inherited dental practice.

A family photograph in a gaudy golden frame sat beside his computer. It was from when his father was still alive, when things were a little happier. It was also evidence Randy had gotten the curse of the old man's ogreish looks, while his brother got the ambition.

He pulled his desk drawer open and reached into the back for his hidden stash of vodka. The first sip truly tasted like rubbing alcohol but the warmth of it snaking down into his stomach eased the anger growing in him.

He often mumbled as he worked, berating himself for becoming his sibling's bitch, for being too quiet and never sticking up for himself. This evening he was silent, his eyes reading over the patient information yet his brain refusing to comprehend it. His brain wanted to be inebriated, to be dazzled by Tanya and her flopping tits.

"Damn it." He rubbed his eyes.

The small flask he hid for emergencies wouldn't be enough, but his salvation was in the back equipment room. Randy promised himself if he just made it through the stack of paperwork before him he would indulge in one of his favorite pastimes, huffing the laughing gas. He scratched his nuts through his slacks, then cracked his knuckles; he meant business.

Hours flew by. He wasn't so sure he actually did everything correctly, but he figured he fucking tried, so that's what really mattered. He fed the papers into the shredder now that the information was stored in his computer. He unbuttoned the top three buttons of his olive green polo shirt. It didn't really match his khaki brown slacks but he wasn't a fashion guru. Any woman who even looked his way only did so because they thought he made the same salary as his wealthy brother.

If they only knew.

He stood up and felt his lower back pop. It was time to chase away the demons of loneliness.

Soon, he'd dragged the nitrous oxide tank out to the patient chair and settled in. His hand searched for a plastic mask in the drawer beside him when—

BOOM!

Startled, Randy spun around to see an orb of blue light dancing in the small hallway outside of the room. It looked like ball lightning and hissed and sizzled with electricity. Randy got to his feet and stood motionless, curious yet scared shitless at the sight. He glanced down at the tank to be certain he hadn't released the gas yet and sent himself into some kind of hallucinations in the cramped room.

The valve was closed; what was taking place had to be reality.

The orb darted toward him, expanding. A figure appeared within the ball of light. Randy felt his bladder threaten to cut loose as hands, studded with teeth, grabbed hold of him.

Then he completely blacked out.

Voices echoed in Randy's foggy mind. A female and a male by the sound of them. He kept his eyes closed but listened to their conversation carefully as his thoughts began to focus.

"Is the human alive?"

"Yes, he lost consciousness but he lives."

"Did he urinate?"

"I'm afraid so, Your Majesty."

As his other senses returned, his nostrils filled with a sickening stench, like that of a burst abscess. He coughed and gagged, spoiling his act of being prostrate.

"He's awakening!"

Randy opened his eyes to bright candle light. His vision fixed first on an arching ceiling adorned with chandeliers. The walls were a shade so familiar to him, he couldn't pinpoint it. Then he noticed his captors looming over him. A scream escaped his dry throat. He forced himself up onto his feet to run, only to find his only way out was blocked by two more figures.

Their faces were vaguely human, yet they were disfigured. Unnaturally enormous mouths split their countenances, teeth protruded from their cheeks and brow lines, and their eyes were bright white. They drew swords and barred the door leading out of the room.

"Leave me alone, you fuckin' freaks!" he cried, his voice breaking like that of a prepubescent boy. Self-consciously, one of his hands dropped in an attempt to hide the warm, wet spot in his pants.

"That's rude!" said the female voice from behind him.

"Especially coming from a grown man who can't control his bladder," the male voice added.

Randy spun to face them. Their faces were the same as the guards with weapons drawn. The woman had auburn hair pinned up in a bun. Beside her stood a muscular man, his long dark hair braided down his back.

"Hyperdontia?" Randy questioned himself aloud, recalling the name of the condition that made people grow extra teeth like great white sharks.

He'd never seen anyone with it so bad, where the teeth actually grew outside the mouth and all over the body. His captors, every one of them, were cases that would grace the covers of dental magazines to display their outrageous disfigurement. He wondered if they hadn't been exposed to radiation, or if they were the outcome of generations of inbreeding.

He brought his free hand up to his own face; relief filled him when he realized his hadn't changed.

"Something like that," the woman answered. Her voice was even and calm now.

Her demeanor soothed him in an odd way. She didn't want to harm him, her posture told him so. She stood unthreatening, her face placid. Tranquility radiated from her, to the point of making Randy wonder if she hadn't put a spell on him.

"Where am I? Who are you?" he asked.

"Welcome to Molarous. I am Queen Bicuspa. In your folklore, I am called the Tooth Fairy."

"Am I dead? I mean, from huffing ...my brother will find my corpse and..."

"Stop this nonsense," said the dark-haired man.

"Easy, Dentin," Bicuspa told him, then returned her attention to Randy.

"You are not deceased. You are very much alive, and after you do as we ask, you will be returned to your world. It was foretold that you are our savior, Dr. Plumber."

"What the fuck are you talking about?" Something in his mind clicked, gears meeting and turning over in his brain. He really felt she meant him no harm, that she was frightened herself and seeking help. But, the Tooth Fairy? Though, if she was, she must have had some sort of magic to ease frightened children if they awakened while she was gathering their teeth.

"How can *I* save you?"

"I recovered your tools," the man called Dentin said. "You are a dentist, are you not?"

"No," Randy said. "That's my brother."

The queen looked stricken. "He's the wrong one!"

She brought her tooth-adorned hand up and covered her tired face, trembling as tears ran from her eyes. "We have failed. We can't risk opening a second portal even if we had a Wisdom to do it."

Randy stood silent, thinking back to the millions of times his brother was the chosen one and not him, over and over again throughout his life. People looked right through him, as if he never existed at all. He felt the queen's heartbreak, the soothing aura she exuded replaced by hopelessness.

Her cries became short painful sobs. The iridescent wings protruding from her back drooped in defeat. She teetered on her feet and Dentin came to catch her before she could fall.

He gently moved her hand away and wiped the tears from her eyes.

"We can't give up now," he whispered.

"I don't know what else we can do. The children ... they are doomed ... their souls..."

"Hush now." Dentin paused in his caresses when he realized all eyes were on them. It was obvious their relationship went beyond a queen and her councilor. Then he placed the back of his hand against her cheek, and fear crept over his already concerned face. "You are feverish."

"I'm only tired."

"Call for Dr. Maxillary at once!" Dentin ordered. The toothy guards ran from the room.

Randy contemplated just hauling ass but was held there by the sight of the queen. She shook now, and from where he stood he saw the hint of something dark at her elbow, like a deep bruise surrounding the random white teeth poking haphazardly through her pale skin.

"May I?" Randy asked, approaching slowly though his brain asked him what the fuck he was doing.

"You said you're not a dentist," Dentin said.

"Not on paper," Randy admitted, "but I *almost* graduated."

A Story of Darkness and Decay

Bicuspa tried to get out of bed but Dr. Maxillary pressed her gently back down. "You must rest."

"My people need me."

"Please," Dentin said.

Randy stood helplessly watching the ailing queen. The dark spot on her arm was already spreading and small yellow pustules were forming. He wrung his hands; his clammy palms reminded him his anxiety was growing. It was the unseen anchor tied about his neck, the reason he had abandoned his schooling.

"Our medical technology has never been tested like this." Maxillary sounded worried. "I warned her to stay out of the infected zone but she wouldn't listen."

Dentin nodded. "Cradling the children, consoling the widows ... but how could we stop her?

"May I have a look?" Randy asked. Seeing the doctor's hesitation, he added, "I practically *am* a dentist."

Maxillary sighed. "I don't see why not. I suppose

your training could be helpful."

"I'll bring the supplies I brought when I…" Dentin said.

"When you kidnapped me?" Randy asked.

"Yes," Dentin admitted. "But it was done for an honorable reason."

Randy was relieved to discover that Dentin had at least cleaned out his supply closet before hauling him to this strange tooth castle expecting him to work miracles. He pulled on latex-free gloves and donned a disposable mask and headlamp. Leaning over the queen, he flipped the bright light on and got a good look at her arm.

Abscesses bubbled all around the teeth protruding from her flesh. Their bases were crusted with yellow buildup. The flesh itself was soft, like gum tissue in an ordinary mouth. Infection turned it a deep red-violet.

"I can lance these, drain them, and clean her teeth," Randy said. "I noticed you brought along some antibiotics as well; I hope your people aren't harmed by them because I can't stop the infection without injecting her with some high powered stuff."

"We rarely have the need for such things," said Maxillary. "This is usually a very healthy kingdom. We brush and floss nightly…"

"Will it harm her?" Dentin asked impatiently.

"Not at all," Maxillary replied. "We often harvest fluorides from the human world, and on occasion, the Wisdoms would procure a dose or two of antibiotics for elderly Hyperdontians. But the disease spreading now is something we've never seen before."

Dentin glowered. "The nameless one."

"The what?" Randy questioned.

"The plague bringer, the malignant entity bent on killing us all and taking access to the portals and the children beyond. That is why you are here."

"Wait, wait, wait. I thought I was going to help make you tooth people healthy again. I'm not a monster fighter."

"You are now, Plumber."

"How the hell do you think I can do that?" He waved his hands before his not-so-manly appearance.

"Do what you can for her, and then you're coming with me, into the infected zone seeking answers," Dentin said.

Randy hesitated but when his eyes fell on the queen, the look of desperation on her pained face, he nodded. "I'll do my best."

Hearing his own words stung his heart. They were his common response to his father, the cold-hearted old man who had adored his brother and always looked on Randy with eyes filled with disappointment.

Streets of Yellow, Bodies of Black

The streets were cobbled with gleaming pearl stones set in a fleshy mortar. Randy could see a yellow buildup gathering around them, as well. It even stretched up the walls of the houses and buildings.

"Plaque?"

"Have you seen it this bad before?" Dentin asked.

"Only in someone's mouth."

They rode horses with bright white coats; their bodies too had extra teeth, making them look like beasts from a childhood nightmare. A small contingency of the queen's men followed.

There was no one out, but citizens peeked from windows as they passed. All bore the same affliction. He cringed involuntarily, but shame replaced it when a small face looked curiously at him. The poor child had teeth protruding from its forehead and its bottom jaw gaped as it struggled to contain the crowded rows of chompers. Randy swallowed in an attempt to wet his dry throat and spoke.

"When did this all start?"

"It's been a fortnight since we found our youngest Wisdom dead," Dentin said."From there, the infection began to spread."

"And this plague bringer? What kind of monster are we talking about, here?"

"I have not laid eyes on the bastard but reports have been passed from the lips of the dying to report his ghastly appearance…like a true demon."

Randy was silent and Dentin seemed to read his thoughts.

"I know you think we are all vile and hideous," he added, "but we are a peaceful people. We are the guardians of your human children."

"I heard the queen mention that, but, how exactly?"

"It's quite simple. When they lose their baby teeth, we gather them and place them in safe keeping so that evil doers like the plague bringer can't get their hands on them."

"And if they did?"

"They would be able to take those little souls for themselves, molding the children into creatures so monstrous and filled with hate that they could destroy your entire world."

Randy was dumbfounded. Though it seemed far-fetched, how could he argue after being brought through a magical portal to the realm of the Tooth Fairy?

"So, how are we gonna stop it?"

"With the brutal force of our fists and swords."

"I don't have a sword."

"But you do have your magic bag."

Randy looked down to the stolen leather satchel embroidered with his brother's initials and felt like a sham all over again.

"I can see the self doubt rising in you," Dentin said."Don't let it take hold of your heart."

Randy Plumber nodded and continued riding onward, his ass growing numb in the uncomfortable saddle.

Dentin halted his horse in front of a two story building. A hanging sign depicted nearly naked women drinking from goblets, all of them decorated with teeth. The windows of the "Pearl Maiden" were of stained glass, the front door of heavy wood with a tiny window set in its center.

"Wait for us here." Dentin ordered his men and motioned Randy down from his horse.

Randy was no prude; he didn't even have to pass the threshold before realizing what kind of place this was.

"Why are we in a whore house?" he asked as they were shown in.

"Just piecing the puzzle together. Don't tell me you are too good to be seen in such a place?" Dentin's comment made Randy feel self-conscious, even though it had merit.

"This ain't my first rodeo; I just didn't see how this was important."

"I'm not here for a brushing, human. I'm here on a

tip, all right?"

"All right…"Randy said, his mind turning over the possible Hyperdontian meaning of "brushing."

They approached a long bar. It was empty, but Randy could tell it was used to being quite busy. The barkeep was a burly old man with a long red beard. His teeth weren't as prominent, but Randy couldn't help staring at a big yellow one protruding from the tip of his bulbous nose.

"Don't stare," Dentin whispered before hailing the owner of the Pearl Maiden.

"Fang."

The gnarled old man nodded and wiped the bar, then sat two cups on its surface. "What'll you be havin'?"

"No drinks, we're here on business. I need to speak with Ivory."

Fang didn't immediately reply, gawking at Randy. Then he stammered a bit and recovered. "Ivory? Oh, yes. Go on upstairs. She hasn't had any customers all day; the plague is really brushin' us all!"

Dentin thanked him and led Randy to the stairwell. "I told you not to stare at his disfigurement, but he couldn't believe yours!"

"I noticed. Talk about awkward."

They made their way to a room at the top of the steps and Dentin knocked on the door.A feminine voice called from inside for them to enter. Randy felt his manhood thrumming with the need to see some flesh and he wasn't disappointed, not entirely. The room was decked out like a French whore house, with grand paintings and a red silk canopy draping over the four post bed. On the crimson sheets lounged a Hyperdontian woman, naked but for her teeth, which didn't cover everything.

"Hello, Ivory. I heard you had some information for me," Dentin said.

"Yes, fair knight." She smiled, playing at being coy, yet Randy could tell she was a really raunchy type by the way she ran her hand down her thigh and spread her legs just enough to reveal teeth replacing where a bush should have been above her vagina.

"You know I don't pay for anything, let alone brushing, so spit it out."

"You're always so prudish, Dentin."

"What did you have to say, Ivory?"

"It's about the witch. The one you have locked up."

Randy could tell this caught Dentin's interest. "Go on," the knight said.

"She was brushing someone out there in the village beyond the gate. Not some farm boy, someone of great importance."

"What proof do you have?"

"The hermit told me. He wanted to floss me in the worst way, but I could tell he was infected." She displayed a thick white thread lying beside her on her bed. Wrapping the floss around her toothy fingers, she pulled it out taut before running it between her pink labia. Ivory sighed and winked at Randy, who felt his trousers growing too tight to contain his growing erection.

"Enough. Tell me what the old man said or be silent," Dentin ordered.

She dropped the act and rose onto her knees. Her heavy breasts hung invitingly, even with a few teeth marring their perfection.

"The witch lived out there in a hut and often called for the assistance of the youngest Wisdom. The pretty one who died not long ago."

"So?"

"They were lovers."

"Many have alluded to that." Dentin sounded exasperated.

"There are books out there in the witch's house. Books of pure evil. Some say the Wisdom gave them to her."

Dentin must have already suspected such news; he bid her a curt good day and turned to leave. Randy found it harder to take his eyes away from the prostitute. He was very curious to see if the act of brushing was any different than the horizontal mambo back on earth. To his disappointment, Dentin's urgent call left no room for letting him find out.

They were back on their horses before Dentin spoke again. "We approach the main gate. Beyond is where the simple folk lived. It's now ravished by plague. We must equip our masks."

He and his men donned face coverings that reminded Randy of something he'd seen in history books, plague doctor's masks with long bird-like noses. Dentin offered one to Randy but he refused. Instead, he dug in his bag of tools and found a disposable mask used when administering dental care.

"Let's be off, then," Dentin said.

A heavy wooden gate was thrown open to reveal the countryside. Rolling hills topped with dead grass and a grey sky filled Randy's vision. Small huts were scattered about, dark and silent on the edge of a great forest. Behind it rose the foothills of a mountain range.

"Our first victim was the youngest of the Wisdoms," explained Dentin as they rode. "A hermit woman beseeched her for help. The Wisdom went to her aid, but came back filled with the rot. We later discovered the one who'd called for help was a sorceress. She is the one who allowed the darkness into Molarous."

"Is she the one Ivory was talking about?"

"Yes, her reputation has spread among the people. If one of them had reported her suspicious behavior months ago, we wouldn't be up to our eyeteeth in dead bodies."

A shadow passed between the hovels, small and childlike. Sadness filled Randy at the thought of some poor little boy or girl forced to live in such a place.

He couldn't believe his eyes as they drew near the outskirts. The sides of the road were lined with ash and bone…and teeth.

"We were ordered to burn the dead," said Dentin, seeing his reaction. "That's another reason we wear these masks. Ours are filled with scented herbs."

"Thanks for telling me sooner, it reeks out here." Randy felt his gut tremble and roll with the onset of nausea.

"Does anyone still live this far from the castle?" he asked in an attempt to put his mind on anything other than the uneasy feeling.

"Not many. Maybe a few who refuse the sanctuary beyond the main gate, like the hermit the whore spoke of. Or those so riddled with disease they were cast out before spreading the plague further."

Remembrance of the tiny shadow gave Randy chills. The little one must have been terrified out there among the wind-scattered piles of ash.

"That's incredibly sad."

"We have no choice until we discover how to kill the infection."

A Hunter from a Coward

"There is the lair of Caries, the witch." Dentin pointed out a hut that had been partially devoured by fire.

"And where is this witch now?" Randy asked. "Ivory said you locked her up?"

"In the dungeons, awaiting execution. We caught her trying to escape into the forest. That's where we suspect her master is hiding."

Randy nodded grimly, cautiously following Dentin up to what seemed to be the starting point of the mysterious sickness. They stopped in front of a charred opening while the queen's guard formed a circle about the scene.

"Look there," Dentin said. "Those are the remains of her books of darkness. We recovered a single text that the Wisdom was trying to decipher…it had magic in it, she was sure of it, the blackest of sorcery. She didn't get to tell us everything before she died." He came close to Randy's ear to add in a whisper, "She too was hiding something. Ivory's information was more than likely correct."

"I'm not sure how I can help with this," Randy said.

"Don't be yellow. Take a good look inside, at the books."

"They're burned."

"Some remain legible in portions."

Shaking his head, Randy stepped into the ruins of the witch's hovel and made his way to the blackened remains of a shelf. It did contain the tattered, burnt pieces of books. To his surprise, they appeared to be modern, from his time, from Earth. He slid a glove onto his right hand and picked up a crumbling volume of dental history.

"What the fuck?"

"What is it, Plumber?"

Randy pried the half ruined book apart and saw clear lines in English.

"This is a book on dentistry.

How did she get it? It's from my world."

A scream shook him and he dropped the book into the black soot at his feet. He retrieved it and shakily opened the satchel to deposit it inside.

Meanwhile, the commotion caused Dentin to spin into action. From his side he drew a long, gleaming white blade. It came to a wicked point like that of an enormous fang.

A horde of small, dark figures rushed from all sides. Their skin was sickly violet, their pores seeping a viscous black substance. Jagged black points of teeth filled their mouths and their eyes bulged like milky yellow bubbles of pus ready to pop.

The horses reared and bucked and tried to flee. Dentin shouted orders, swinging his sword with deadly precision, cutting several of the creatures in two. The guards rallied even as their foes launched at them, jaws-first. As some of the injured men fell, the creatures ripped the bird-like masks from their faces and vomited dark fluid into their screaming mouths.

The reek was so terrible Randy's stomach leapt into his throat. It was like drilling straight into a cavity-riddled molar, but to the hundredth power. A shuffling behind him told him he was not alone. His heart stuttered as he spun to see one of the vile little bastards had crept into the half-burnt house behind him. It grinned, baring its hideous maw of rot. As the beast jumped forward, ready to bite a chunk out of him, his hand dove into his bag and produced a single sharp pick used for cleaning teeth. Randy jammed the shining steel utensil into the creature's eye, then yanked it free. Yellow chunks erupted, splattering his arm. The monster fell back and Randy kicked it through the scorched, crumbling wall. It retreated with a single eye to guide it.

Randy staggered from shock, the violence and close combat too much for him. The stench triggered something in his brain.

"They're full of disease!" he shouted, yanking his bag open; in the bottom of it were a few bottles of mouthwash. He opened one and dumped it on his hand and arm to cleanse it of the yellow chunks left behind.

Opening two more of them, he ran to the men who'd been forced to ingest the vomitous plague.

They were clearly already ill, and he wasted no time pouring the mouthwash, instructing them to gargle and spit. As they did so, he popped open a bottle of antibiotics and began forcing pills down their throats.

"What the devil were those?" asked Dentin, approaching as the last of the hideous creatures fell or fled.

"I was hoping you'd know," Randy said.

"I've never witnessed anything so evil." Wiping his sword, he nodded toward his men. "Will they live?"

"I think so, but would advise them to see Dr. Maxillary."

Once the soldiers were on their feet again, Dentin dispatched them back to the castle.

Randy sighed with relief and pulled the stained mask from his face, making to follow. He took a step after the retreating guards, only to have Dentin grip his shoulder.

"Not you, dentist. We're going hunting."

The dungeon smelled of fetid breath. A constant drip in the distance kept Caries awake.

She had stopped tallying the days on the yellowed walls after six passed. Her heart hurt that her lover was gone, but the rest of the bastards she'd enjoy watching rot away.

Hammaspeikko would make them all pay, and she would be granted freedom for her loyalty.

She ran her fingers through her greasy black hair and

tugged free a few strands. She sat braiding them together, waiting.

She would be the queen of a new earth, as her master promised. She only wished Succedanea were still alive ... not only for the lustful affair they'd carried on together, but for, the young Wisdom's power to open the portal to Earth.

The demon king sought to open that doorway again, to roam freely amongst the weak breed known as humanity; she desired to help him accomplish that. Peering up at the tiny, barred window at the top of her cell wall, she cast out what meager magic she still had, and cursed as it waned.

"One still lives, a hidden one...another Wisdom," she said in a whisper.

Something else registered on the periphery of her magical net; the one who would no doubt come for her. Then the spell faded completely, leaving her frustrated that she couldn't scry any further but also hopeful that her destiny would soon be fulfilled.

The image in her mind was of a demon in fluttering black robes, his mouth parting and black fire consuming the pearly white castle.

Dr. Maxillary, Max as he was known by many of his patients, sat by candle light. He inspected the work the dentist had performed, nodding in approval. The queen's wounds were open yet hadn't gathered anymore pus in the hours since Randy lanced the abscesses and administered antibiotics.

A racket beyond the door drew his attention, the voices of men talking excitedly. The doctor made his way out to find the queen's guards had returned, all of them looking quite peaked.

"What is going on here?" he asked.

"We were attacked," one of the guards answered.

A second guard spoke up. "These things spat their vile evil into our faces, but the dentist, he helped us."

"We need you to monitor us," added the first. "Lord Dentin commands it."

Dr. Max knew their story had to be the truth just by looking at their stained tunics and pale faces.

"This way. Go quickly and wash up, then change your clothing. I will watch over you as instructed."

Dentin and Randy followed the path of yellow fluid left behind by one of the fleeing creature. It led into a copse of leaf-bare trees. The forest seemed to be in hibernation, or possibly it was autumn in Molarous. The bark of the trees was riddled with random toothy growths and even the mushrooms gathering about their roots were shaped like molars.

When Dentin halted and looked over to Randy Plumber, he was noticeably frightened.

"Steel your nerves, dentist."

Randy gulped but only nodded in response before he followed Dentin into the trees.

"I can smell him," Dentin said, voice low

"Me too, it's like terrible halitosis."

Their feet crunched upon the dead leaves no matter how stealthily they attempted to proceed. The silence was smothering. Randy could almost sense the beast watching them, plotting to attack. It was small but its mouth full of rot, its infectious bite, and its horrible oily skin made up for its stature.

There was a rustling of leaves as a brown-grey blur startled them. A squirrel paused on the gnarled bark of a tree, body cruelly beleaguered by rows of tiny sharp teeth protruding through its soft fur. It darted away into the silent forest.

Dentin cursed. Then

his face twisted in horror and Randy knew their prey had become their hunter.

Everything happened with such speed that Randy only fell back screaming as the goblin-like beast leapt from its hiding spot. Dentin spun, lashing out with his blade, but missed the small toothy projectile. He only barely managed to turn his head in time, face avoiding the festering maw. It latched onto his ear instead, removing it in a single bite. The Hyperdontian warrior screamed as his flesh tore free in the fangs of the monster. The thing was no bigger than a child yet it bit with the ferociousness of a juvenile shark. Blood poured in a river down the side of his head and stained his royal garb.

"You little bastard!" he raged, and whipped his sword back in an upward arc that caught the infectious troll in the groin. The blade cleaved upward into its belly. The creature quivered as its stinking lifeblood tainted the ivory sword.

Randy felt disgust rushing through him as its ocular cavity continued to spill a yellow substance the color and consistency of lemon pudding down its grotesque face.

"Master will kill you all." It spoke in a gravelly voice.

"Who sent you?" Dentin asked.

The creature coughed and wheezed but did nothing but smile defiantly.

"Who brought you here?"

When it refused to respond, Dentin gripped the sword still lodged in the troll's lower abdomen and began to pull it upward. The creature cried out, helpless as the blade traveled through its tender flesh.

"Who?"

"Hammaspeikko."

"Keep speaking gibberish while I cut you in two, then I'll cut your tiny goblin cock off and force it down your throat!"

"NO! Hammaspeikko *is* my master!" it whined.

The word meant nothing to Randy, and Dentin didn't seem to recognize it either, though he stored it away for later. With a powerful jerk, Dentin pulled his blade upward and cut the pitiful beast in two. Its severed innards spilled out in separate piles as the stink of it filled the lonesome forest.A fragment of vengeance for all who had suffered from the plague.

"On your feet," he said, turning to Randy.

"Where are we going now?" Randy asked.

"To the dungeon to speak with the witch. I'm positive she will know what that piece of shit meant." He motioned to the dead creature before cleaning his blade on the bottom of his stained tunic.

"Wait," Randy said and opened his bag. "Let me treat that bite."

Dentin nodded, remembering his missing ear, and took a seat on a tree stump.

Randy found a bottle of fluoride and doused the side of Dentin's head, eliciting a hiss as the minty liquid served as an antiseptic. Randy then drew a dose of antibiotics into a needle and stuck it in the wound.

"I might still have my ear if you hadn't have swooned like a woman." Dentin huffed.

"Hey, sorry; I'm not used to this!"

"We have no time for cowardice. I have no idea how you lived in your world, but here, it is kill or be killed."

Randy remained silent as he returned the fluoride and antibiotics to his bag, his brother's bag. His fingers hesitated over the golden stitching, where his brother's initials stood out boldly against the black leather.

"To the castle with all haste," Dentin said as he got up.

Randy hurried after the warrior who had made it his mission to become the salvation of all the tooth people. Maybe the Hyperdontians had no idea of the entity responsible for their plight, but the name alone made Randy nearly shit himself.

Their horses were still nowhere in sight, so they had to proceed on foot. Randy struggled to keep up with the fit toothy armored warrior. He never worked out, though he wasn't necessarily obese, just flabby. His fitness routine usually consisted of walking from his car to the front desk of the dental office.

By the time the castle walls were in view, the scent of burning filled their nostrils and the sounds of screaming filled their ears. Any hope that resided in their hearts died with the vision of smoke and fire.

"The queen!" Dentin cried, and took off running toward the great gates of Molarous.

They ran up the rutted road between the small huts on the outskirts of the city. A scream caused Randy to glance back. On their heels came a mass of oily trolls, their faces fixed in grim grins, bent on destruction.

A young woman fled one of the darkened houses, her golden hair fluttering as if in slow motion as Randy watched. A group of creatures bounded to overtake her. Dentin was completely fixated on getting back into the burning ivory city and paid no attention to the screaming damsel. Randy knew he could no longer hesitate so he ran towards the girl as she fell beneath a mass of snapping black teeth.

He equipped himself with a bottle of fluoride and spun the cap hastily before dousing the creatures like a priest casting holy water.

It contacted their skin, hissing and bubbling as it ate into them, and as one they whirled to face this unlikely would-be hero.

Breath of Fire and Disease

The stricken girl cast dazzling blue eyes up at him, tears streaming down her cheeks. Randy stood firm, wielding his bottle of fluoride, driving the demons back. Inch by inch they retreated. Then sudden fear fell over their terrible faces. Some even fled back into the shadows gathering beside the abandoned huts.

Randy felt pride swelling within him until he heard the battle cry from behind. Dentin had returned, his white blade flashing in the falling sunlight as he fought off the last of the attackers. That was what they had feared; that was what had made them flee.

A faltering touch at his knee made him look down; the girl had her hand extended. He helped her to her feet, thinking he should say something brave or clever and unable to come up with a thing.

"Let's go!" Dentin cried, racing for the gates with Randy and the girl following.

They entered the once dazzling city to be met by

flames and a great commotion. Houses burned as citizens flooded the white-cobbled streets. Fang came from his establishment, wielding an ax handle, total disbelief painting his haggard face.

"What is happening here?" Dentin asked him.

"Haven't a clue," Fang replied. "There was a terrible sound like that of booming thunder, but greater, and the air filled with smoke."

Ivory ran out, wrapped in red silk. Her usually playful attitude had dissipated. "A monster!" she cried, seizing Dentin by the shoulder. "A monster like a storm cloud came over the city in a fury. Faster than anything I've ever seen, headed for the castle. I saw it, Dentin. I saw it!" She began to weep, but the knight brusquely freed himself from her grasp and continued to run for the white castle.

"Bicuspa!" he called, voice wracked with desperation and fear.

Randy, still holding the girl's hand, guided her along with him as they made their way to the castle. It had clearly been under attack. A gaping hole reduced one wall to rubble, while the others were sullied with black smoke and soot.

Dentin, heedless, rushed up the grand steps and into the gritty, billowing, dark clouds. Randy stopped, aware of a smell, the distinct stench of rotted gums, but at a magnitude he'd never experienced in all his years of dentistry. His gorge threatened to rise in his throat, the overwhelming urge to puke turning his skin cold and clammy.

"It's burning," the girl said softly. Randy squeezed her hand supportively.

"You're hurt," he said, indicating the side of her neck, which bled from the raking teeth of her attackers.

"I'm just happy to be alive." She smiled sadly. "Thank you."

"I was just doing my duty." The words slipped out before he could calculate their cheese factor, but she beamed up at him.

He realized as he finally got a good look at her that her face bore none of the afflictions of her fellow countrymen. No extra teeth protruded from her flesh. Her skin was flawless.

She blushed and shyly turned away from his gaze, almost as if embarrassed.

"I, uh, should see to those wounds before they get infected," he said.

Ducking her head, she nodded and murmured another quiet, "Thank you."

They waited in a slightly awkward silence. After what felt like an eternity, Dentin returned, his face grim.

"The witch has escaped," he announced. "The queen survived the assault, but Caries is gone, absconded with the nameless one responsible for all this."

"What do we do now?" Randy asked.

"Follow me. The doctor wants to speak to you."

They hurried into the ravaged castle to find Dr. Maxillary waiting for them.

"Your solution worked so far," he said. "The guards did not get infected."

Randy felt relief wash over him. For once, he had done something right. "If we get some fluoride on the attacked before the infection truly sets in, it could save lives."

"Thank the gods we found you," the doctor said.

Relieved though he was that the soldiers hadn't fallen ill, he knew his bag didn't hold enough mouthwash or antibiotics for the entire city. It worried him. He saw the damsel gazing at him with hope burning in her eyes.

"Come, young lady, allow me to treat you," he said, and she nodded.

As he examined her, he marveled again at the condition of her skin. Pale and smooth, not a tooth to be seen.

She, in turn, seemed to be studying him. "You're not from here, are you?" she asked.

"How could you guess?"

"You're different, like me."

"Oh, yes, I'm from Earth"

"That's what I suspected."

"Do you know much of my world?"

"Only from what I heard from the young Wisdom, when she used to come to the outskirts. Before she died, before the witch killed her. At least, that's what my father said, that her love for the witch brought her a painful end."

"I'm sorry," Randy said.

"I suppose that is the fate of those who consort with evil."

"I suppose so."

"Do the others call you a freak? Like they have me my whole life?"

"You wouldn't be called that in my world!" he blurted. "Men would worship you."

She smiled, but it was the sort of dubious, polite smile of someone unaccustomed to compliments. Embarrassed, Randy busied himself administering a pink, bubblegum-flavored fluoride rinse to her wounds. She winced as the solution flooded her shallow lacerations.

"Sorry," he said. "I'm sure that stings."

"Much better than rotting away," she replied. "Like the others ... like my father."

Her confession gutted Randy; it broke his heart in an instant, provoking him to make a promise to her.

"I will care for you if you have no one else."

Her soft hand gripped his gloved one; she caressed it. "Thank you, stranger."

"My name is Randy." He smiled behind his disposable face mask.

"Mine is Gingiva. My father raised me; he was all that I had. He used to tell me one day I would find a good man and we would marry, live the rest of our lives together. I never used to believe him ... you know, with my freakish appearance and all ... but now I do."

Randy's heart fluttered, he wasn't accustomed to such tenderness. His usual encounters with the opposite sex were not what he would call a voluntary reciprocation of affection; it usually came with a price tag. He found himself wanting to lean over and kiss her on the top of her perfect head, to smell her silken blond hair, to inhale that scent of her and never release it.

Then Dentin burst through the door, interrupting the magical moment he was having with the beautiful Gingiva.

"The witch Caries was extracted from the dungeon by the demon himself," Dentin reported. "The guards down below are all eaten up with the sickness. He set part of the keep on fire, along with pieces of the city in his escape. Those trolls, their powers are nothing compared to their master's. The sickness he wields takes over the body instantly."

"How are we going to stop this?" Randy asked.

"Any way that we can. We have no choice. The children depend on us."

Randy nodded in silent agreement. He couldn't allow the kids of his world to be taken over by the monster ravaging the tooth kingdom.

"He is powerful indeed, and he's up to something. I have my suspicions," Dentin said. "There is one thing in this whole kingdom that any one of us would die for rather than give it away. Even the queen herself would undergo a torturous death before revealing it."

"What would that be?"

"The White Hoard of Molarous."

Randy stood over the queen, whose health was taking a

definite downward spiral.

She was sweating, the skin of her face as white as the teeth decorating it Even her large lips were colorless. He'd had so much hope for her, but now he felt as if he was watching her wither away.

As he fetched a dose of antibiotics and administered it to her frail arm, his mind wandered through his years of dental training. He'd read about gum disease. The worst of it was devastating. There were many walk-in patients who came to see his brother to end their pain, their faces swollen and their gums so infected he could smell it on their breath from across the front counter. It was nothing compared to this.

He recalled the book confiscated from the witch's hovel. He pulled it from his bag and sat beside the window. The smell of fire and halitosis still hung in the air; beneath it lingered the scent of terror. He flipped the book open and thumbed through its half-burnt pages.

Why would a witch need a book from his world?

His eyes roved over the words. Most of what he could decipher was about ancient dental practices. Then he spotted a garbled word, a name, the same that the creature in the trees had spoken … Hammaspeikko. Randy grabbed a candle and held it over the page. There were only a few sentences about the plague bringer, but they chilled him to his dental-school-dropout bones.

It all made sense. The Hyperdontians were on the right path in their assumptions about the nameless one. He was after their hoard of baby teeth. He was a demon who hunted Earth children's pearly whites, but for centuries he had been banished.

Handwritten notes gave away the plot constructed by not just the witch, but the young Wisdom herself as well.

We shall leave this tiny kingdom. He has promised it. If we release him, he shall compensate us. We shall be the queens of New Earth. No one can stop us. Our power will be immeasurable and our love will last ages.

Dentin entered the room. "She is resting, the girl you saved."

Randy closed the book. "I've found something. You were right, and so was Ivory. The young Wisdom was in on the plot to bring that demon here."

"I suspected as much. Only Wisdoms can open the portals. I didn't believe she was tricked. The little rat only came crawling back to the castle for medical attention."

"But you said there are no more Wisdoms, so how can the demon and the witch even make it to Earth?"

"No more Wisdoms that we are aware of," Dentin said. "But there is always one in this kingdom, somewhere, maybe only a babe suckling its mother's tit as we speak."

"How could a baby open a portal?" Randy scoffed.

"They can't, but their blood and teeth could be used to do so," Dentin answered grimly.

So, it wasn't only the children of Earth in danger, but any of those poor kids out there in the streets of Molarous.

"How can we know who is the next one?" Randy asked.

"They are overcome with a change. The Wisdoms are more adorned than the rest of us. When they are teething their armor, it's agonizing."

Randy nodded, contemplating the tremendous pain one would endure to push forth an entire suit of teeth from their skin. He shivered.

Dentin moved to the queen's bedside. "She appeared to be feeling better before, but now she looks so weak."

"Some infections of the gums are more serious than others, and depending upon the patient's health, can last a long time," Randy said. "Such as necrotizing ulcerative gingivitis, also called NUGS or trench mouth."

"Is that what is eating us all alive?"

"It seems similar, but NUGS isn't contagious. This is something much more dangerous, something supernatural."

"What can be done?" Dentin asked, gazing at the unconscious Bicuspa.

"I have to treat every case to the best of my abilities," Randy said. "And destroy the monster that brought it here."

His mind conjured the countenance of an old black and white vampire movie he'd watched the evening before he came to Molarous. *Dark Night of the Nosferatu.* He'd laughed at how ridiculous the plotline was at the time, but now he found himself in a real life creature feature.

"Could it be the plague won't end until we kill the plague bringer himself?" Dentin asked.

It was a question that had just begun to blossom in

Randy's own mind as well.

"There's only one way to find out."

Going back to his leather satchel,

he rifled through it in hopes of locating a tool his brother often used in the treatment of trench mouth. But it was nowhere to be seen. He wanted to slam his head against the wall in disappointment.

"What's the matter, dentist?"

"There was one more thing I wanted to test on the queen. I think it would at least stave off her infection until we can get rid of this Hammaspeikko."

Teething

Her master paced in the absence of light, his eyes able to see all even when hers could not. He had taken to a cave in the mountain range while his children spread their disease among the helpless tooth people.

When he'd learned of her imprisonment, he had bided his time, allowing the defending army to grow weak before striking and reclaiming her from the dungeon.

"We shall claim the next Wisdom," Caries said. "I could feel her there close to the city."

"Then the portal will be opened, and my time on Earth will come once more." His voice was a rasping nightmare.

The stink of him would have turned anyone's stomach; even Caries had to steel herself in order to not offend the great Hammaspeikko. He smelled of the rotten breath of a corpse, a pungent stench so foul and repugnant that it hung in the air like campfire smoke and left the taste of literal shit on Caries's tongue.

Nor was he any better to look upon, making her almost grateful for the darkness of the cave. He stood larger than any grown man, at least by a head or more. Black and filthy robes hung in tattered pieces from his body, exposing flesh riddled with pustules. Abscesses rose in great yellow mountains across his long nose and pointed chin. A yellowed beard wrapped around his head and blended into the dreadlocked mass of hair he kept tied with a strip of leather.

About his neck hung a cord strung with tiny teeth, his conquests from the past. He fidgeted with the necklace, though the magic in the baby teeth had been expended ages before. This was why he'd sought the aid of Caries and her now-dead lover. The stash of pearly whites, the stockpiled treasure of Molarus, was nearly mythological in scale. He'd spent centuries seeking the kingdom of the Tooth Fairy from his exile in the void between worlds.

Now he had found it at last.

Luckily for Hammaspeikko, there were those weak enough in Molarous to fall for his guile and empty promises.

He turned to regard Caries. It amused him whenever he encountered fools like her. She was willing to destroy her own people for her own selfish gains, to wear the sash of Earth's queen, though it would surely be in ruins before she could even celebrate her coronation.

He had spent hundreds of years upon that world,

wreaking havoc and turmoil wherever he roamed, but his long banishment made him wish only to destroy every man, woman and child on the face of the planet in one fell swoop of rancid disease.

And to claim their children's souls while they died in torment. There would be no greater vengeance recorded.

"Cast your magic out," he told the witch. "Find the next tooth hag. Once I've claimed the hoard, we'll need her to open the door."

"Yes, master."

His trolls entered the cave, answering his mental summons. He pointed to the black wall behind him and they dove into their work, using their hands and sometimes their hideous mouths to break through the dirt and rock. They would dig, would tunnel their way through, and this last barrier keeping him from the tooth kingdom's most prized and sacred possession would fall.

The teeth of Earth's children soon would be his.

"With no Wisdoms in our court," said Dentin, as they sat in the light of a dying candle, "we can't access your world. We haven't been able to collect the children's precious teeth in weeks. Our legacy will fade from them and they will grow cold and jaded much too early in life."

"We can't allow that to happen." Randy thought back on his own childhood; things like the Tooth Fairy and Santa Claus were happy memories for him, some of the few he treasured.

"It is our purpose to keep them filled with hope and joy," Dentin went on. "That in turn spreads an everlasting feeling of youth to the people here. Our queen is over three hundred years old; I can't bear to watch her fade away."

Bicuspa coughed, drawing their attention. Dentin and Randy went to her side.

She looked up at them. "I don't know what magic you wrought, dentist, but I can feel my body fighting."

"Rest, Your Majesty." Randy said.

"No, you must listen to me." She spoke with an effort, her body trembling. "We must find the next Wisdom and protect the hoard. The demon will seek them out."

Dentin lifted her delicate hand in his and knelt beside her bed. "You have my vow, my lady."

"How can we possibly find the next Wisdom?" Randy asked.

"There is always one," she answered. "Out there, somewhere amidst the chaos."

"And the hoard?" He still wasn't quite sure how a bunch of baby teeth could be so important.

Dentin spoke for her as the queen fell back onto her pillow. "A stash much more valuable than all the gold and jewels of every world combined, the currency of happiness and hope. It sustains us all."

"Where is it? Not here in the castle, I'm guessing." The sheer size of it alone must be mind-boggling. Twenty baby teeth per child, millions of children over hundreds or thousands of years ... magnificent, like a sea of tiny pearls.

"In the mountains beyond the forest. We must defend it to the death."

"We *must*," Bicuspa reiterated, feverish mind struggling against its battle to stay awake. "It's one of the components the beast will require if he wishes to walk in your world again."

"And the teeth of a Wisdom," Randy mused.

A scream broke the building anticipation between them. Dentin gripped his sword and ran for the door. Randy pulled a dental pick from his bag and followed the ivory knight down the hallway. His heart beat frantically as they drew near the very room he'd treated Gingiva in.

"The girl!" Dentin said.

They entered, expecting to find a handful of the tooth goblins assailing her. What they found was that Gingiva had stripped off all of her clothes. Her skin was slick with sweat. It oozed from her pores and drenched her sheets.

"The sickness must have taken hold of her." Dentin sheathed his sword.

Gingiva writhed on the bed, screaming, tormented by absolute agony. Randy pushed past the unnerved guard and rushed to her side, though with no idea what to do when he got there.

"None of the infected have reacted this way," Dentin said in terrified wonder.

Her eyes were tightly shut as if in concentration, as if attempting to weather the storm of pain ripping its way through her nerves. She screamed again, long and ragged.

"Gingiva?" Randy asked.

Dr. Maxillary had joined them but didn't dare approach, speaking from the doorway.

"Since she is a ... since she's... like you, is it possible the infection is different in her body?"

"She's not a freak!" Randy snapped over her pitiful shrieks.

Suddenly, her flesh began to split open, lines of blood running down her body from every pore. Randy stumbled back in shock.

"By the gods!" the doctor shouted. "The virus must have mutated!"

Randy felt tears welling up in his eyes. The kindness, and even affection she had shown him were something he cherished deeply even after only knowing her for a span of hours. Seeing her like this, with the blood and the agonized cries, was too much to bear. He brought his hand to his mouth to stifle the sobs that clawed up his throat. It didn't work. He broke down, weeping like a child.

"Put her out of her misery!" Dentin said. Pushing Randy aside, he raised his blade. In a single stroke, he meant to remove her head and end her suffering completely.

As Dentin steadied himself, casting a pitying gaze down on her one last time, he caught his breath and halted. Tears of his own sprang to his eyes. He turned to Randy and Max.

"Look!" he gasped. "This is no plague!"

They edged closer. There amidst the blood were

thin white lines, pearly and abundant in Gingiva's flesh. Randy hiccoughed, still crying uncontrollably, wiping at snot dangling from his nostrils. He tried to form questions but only managed a confused blubbering.

"You're right, Dentin!" the doctor exclaimed."SHE'S TEETHING!"

"Whuh-what?" sniveled Randy.

"In all my years, I've never personally witnessed the sacred transformation! She's the next Wisdom!"

"The last hope of the kingdom, right here within the walls of the castle!" Dentin exulted. "Fate smiles upon the people of Molarous and our queen!"

Maxillary shook himself and regained professionalism. "Gather some clean towels! Dentist, any pain medication you might have!"

Weeping again, this time in relief, Randy ran down the hall to retrieve his bag.

He found a single tube of numbing gel and a bottle of high powered pain killers. He brought the leather satchel back to the waiting doctor and joined him in administering aid to Gingiva.

They watched as her flesh opened and pushed forth rows upon rows of teeth. She trembled and continued to cry out weakly as the transformation swept over her body.

Randy felt a pang of guilt, he had called the Hyperdontians freaks when he was first pulled through the portal, but to him she was still the most beautiful thing he'd ever seen. The dentist in him wanted to covet her, polish every one of her pearly white studs and floss between each one.

Finally, she lay still and her breathing began to even out. She opened her eyes; the blue irises had gone completely white. She opened her mouth to speak but couldn't muster a single sentence.

"Everything is going to be just fine," Randy said, leaning over her.

A tear ran from the corner of her eye and trailed its way between the rows of teeth that replaced the smooth plain of her cheek.

"I'm ... a monster." She finally spoke, her gaze falling on her exposed flesh that was now riddled with teeth.

"No," he said. "No, you are the most beautiful thing in the entire kingdom, at least to me."

She attempted to smile, but the lidocaine in her muscles only allowed a partial grin on one side while the other hung unmoving.

"Really?" she mumbled.

He nodded and gently kissed her toothy forehead as her eyes drifted closed

"Randy." Dentin beckoned him to the door. "You must guard her with every drop of your blood, with every breath in your lungs, every beating of your heart. For she is one of the keys the demon seeks."

Randy nodded. "I will guard her with my life."

"I must gather my men and go to fortify the treasure," Dentin said solemnly.

Randy could feel the electric impatience of impending violence. War was on the smoke-choked horizon and they all had to prepare themselves. The queen's guard was obviously exhausted but refused to allow it to affect him. This was not the hour for weakness.

"Be vigilant, dentist." Dentin saluted, then exited the room in haste.

The White Hoard

The tunnel bit deep into the mountain, the trolls acting much like burrowing worms. They consumed the dirt and shit it out in thin pools of blackened stool.

Their master followed contentedly behind. He had already sent the witch to find the Wisdom; the two keys would soon be in place to open the portal.

He stopped to taste the air. It was dense with the rapid breaths of his children and fouled by their feces but he could still decipher the hint of something else. The essence of childhood played over his tongue, of sweets and bubblegum-flavored toothpaste, of chocolate ice cream and endless dreaming. His ancient heart thudded wildly in his chest.

Victory was within reach! After so many lifetimes of being lost in utter darkness, feeling his way around like a blind grub, he would soon walk in the sunshine of Earth once more. The void in which he'd spent his imprisonment would pale in comparison to the ruins he planned to make of the human world. Their own children would become their executioners, tiny armies of the possessed flooding the world in blood and tears. And he would be their commander.

His gnarled face twisted into a grin as his trolls declared that they were within a few yards of breaching the chamber. He reminded himself to remain patient, something he had learned while drifting in the blackness between the worlds. He would bide his time and strike with the speed and force of a serpent the size of the cosmos.

He was ready; his time had come at last.

Caries knew she was weakened by the loss of her magical charms, but also by the loss of her lover, the young Wisdom who'd been destined to take the place of the aging tooth hag before her.

Succedanea had been an alluring thing, a Wisdom by blood, yet something in her was tainted from the moment she breached her mother's womb. The great energy coursing beneath her toothy adornment only increased the interest Caries felt. An interest that proved mutual, as well as useful.

After a torrid affair, she'd agreed to open the door to earth for Caries. The witch had landed in a library in the middle of the night, and, as fate would have it, the first book she absconded with back to her realm was one all about ancient dentistry. Within those yellowed pages she learned of the great Hammaspeikko and his banishment, in the darkest ages when the young queen was still at her mother's breast.

Communing with him had required much power, more than she had within her. It was her lover once more who came to her aid. The arduous ritual lasted nearly three days, Caries extracting teeth from Succedanea's flesh to keep the gate to the void open. The Wisdom was left nearly naked, covered with gaping holes from the procedure.

The tooth demon had roared through the doorway in a burst of black fire, bringing infectious clouds in his wake. His foul children were birthed right there on the wooden floor of her hovel, spit out of the undulating rift, dripping viscous black oil and crying for something to appease their aching stomachs. The bustling city outside called to them, and they went to feed.

Succedanea fled in the middle of the night, her betrayal leaving Caries heartbroken. Only later, when everyone around her began to sicken and die, did she guess the fate that must have befallen her lover. She herself was protected by the demon as long as she did his bidding, but her neighbors were not so fortunate. Her home had caught fire as they burned the corpses of their kin; perhaps it had been an accident, perhaps not.

She and her master had escaped into the forest. He sent his children out to infect more of the weaklings of Molarous, and rapidly the Hyperdontians fell.

He thus far had kept his bloody promises to her. Now, with nothing else to live for, she continued to follow him down his path of diseased conquest. Her heart ached, guilt gnawing at her hollow interior, but she wished to fill it with supreme power in hopes it would chase away the memory of dooming the beautiful Wisdom to a horrible death. On Earth, she would have unlimited magic, be a queen of darkness. It emboldened her the way the thought of fresh meat might coax a starving animal.

Caries still had small bursts of magic left in her, which she used now to hone in on the heartbeat of one in tremendous pain, one undergoing the transformation. She crept to the gates of Molarous as a flood of workers came out to discard the bodies of those who died in the throes of sickness. Their carts brimmed over with the dead, laden with women, men, and even infants.

It took everything in her to turn her face away from a free meal. Babies had the tenderest flesh that could pass the foul lips of someone such as herself. Ignoring the hunger pains and angry growls of her stomach, she slipped into the panicked city. The scent of fire was still very much present, an aftermath of her escape. The vision of the plague bringer in all his hideous resplendence casting a ball of black fire at the ivory wall of the castle was something she'd never forget.

For days, she'd wondered if her loyalty would be forgotten, but it hadn't been, and her payment would soon be collected. All she had to do now was find the new Wisdom and yank the teeth from her flesh.

Caries grinned wickedly beneath the hood of a cloak she kept wound about her. Citizens rushed by her in droves, all stricken numb by fear and paying no attention to the viper winding her way through their midst. She froze when she realized the signaling heartbeat she kept in her subconscious rang out from the castle, the very place in which she was formerly imprisoned.

She would have to be all the more cunning and wary to accomplish this task, for her magic was now almost spent. The last of her power spoke to her, guiding her gaze to a window in a pearly tower at the heart of the castle. The Wisdom was in that room, birthing a set of armor from her pores and gaining the majestic power within her blood.

The witch retreated into the shadows as the sound of footsteps, a hundred strong, came marching from the elaborate entryway to the fairy queen's home. Blending into the darkness, she watched the soldiers pass by, no doubt making their way to the chamber hidden in the mountain.

She grinned, knowing her master would be there to greet them.

Randy sat in a wooden chair beside Gingiva. She was sleeping as comfortably as she could after her ordeal.

The doctor had covered her in a thin sheet to keep her once nude body concealed. It was now covered in rows of radiant white teeth; only the soles of her feet, her eyelids, nipples, and lips remained the flawless skin of her former self. Her golden hair remained vibrant and shining; it waved down around her shoulders and covered the pillow placed beneath her head.

Randy couldn't help but gaze upon her form, barely masked, and find her absolutely stunning. He wanted to whisper to her just how beautiful she was, but he didn't want to frighten her with his forwardness. Instead, he watched the slow rise and fall of her breathing and the now placid look on her face.

The pain she had endured could have killed her, but she'd pulled through. If what Dentin said was true, she would become a highly respected figure among the Hyperdontians. It soothed Randy's mind a bit to know she would be appreciated and protected, but it caused him great fear to think of what the demon and the witch would do if they got their hands on her.

He opened his bag and pulled out the tattered book to read while he sat guard over the sleeping Wisdom. He came back to the handwritten message beside the name of the plague bringer and his mind went back to his conversation with Dentin about trench mouth and NUGS. It dawned on him that, with Gingiva's help, he could slip back into Jerry's dental practice and bring back a weapon so powerful that no infection could withstand it. The Laser Light 2000.

She sighed and her eyes opened. Her head turned towards him and to his amazement she spoke.

"Randy."

"Gingiva, I'm here."

"I ... I'm changed."

"Yes. You're radiant."

"I heard you telling me so," she said, smiling faintly. Seeing his evident confusion, she added,

"I can read your thoughts. Don't ask me how; I guess it's something I can do now that I've changed."

"I'll try to keep my thoughts as pure as possible, then," he teased, earning a soft laugh from her.

"You're exhausted. You should rest."

"No."

"Gingiva, I don't want you to exert yourself." He took her tooth-studded hand in his. "Sleep, and I'll watch over you."

"But I could hear you thinking about a weapon. I want to help you retrieve it."

"This is all new to you. I don't want to hurt you."

"New, but natural," she replied. "Since my body transformed, I understand. Like instinct. Like how a bird learns to fly."

"I'm not so sure we should risk it."

"I'm already at risk. Someone hunts me...she is close."

He paused then stood, clenching his fists.

"Her breath is like a hungry animal, seeking my blood," Gingiva said. "She will not be swayed. You have to stop her."

"What if I can't?" He heard his own fear and it mortified him, but the words kept spilling out.

"My whole life, I've been a disappointment, a joke." His mind flooded with memories of his father, his brother, his failures, his shame."I'm not the hero you think I am."

"Those who made you feel otherwise were foolish," Gingiva said. "I can see your heart now. I know who you are. You are the hero I need, that Molarous needs. You can do this."

Her words nearly brought him to tears.

Raising her slim arm, she asked, "Do you have anything to extract one of these with?"

"Wait, you mean yank one of those out?" Randy asked.

"Yes. It's like a picture in my mind, showing me what to do. There was another Wisdom here, in this castle. She died, but in some way she's showing me what to do, passing her knowledge to my body."

Extraction

Randy opened his dental bag and rummaged around inside. His fingers brushed against the stainless steel forceps his brother used to pry teeth from many patients. He didn't know if he had it in him to yank one free from Gingiva's soft skin.

"I will do it," she said.

"The whole mind reading thing again?"

He placed the forceps in her palm and stood back, not really knowing what to expect.

Her hand rose into the air, moving in a sequence of triangular shapes. Randy felt a pop of static electricity that raised his hackles and the hair on his arms. He watched Gingiva touch the pair of shining forceps to her wrist. The teeth there were small, like those of a child. She gripped one and began to pull. Her arm trembled as she expended her strength to pry the tooth free of her skin; blood ran from the open hole left behind.

A blue orb of light flickered into being before them

as she winced and exhaled. Randy recognized it as nearly identical to the one he'd seen when he was brought through.

"I, the Wisdom of Molarous, seek this Earth dentist's place of employment…" She hesitated a moment, as if listening to instructions from an inaudible voice. "Open the gate between worlds for Randy Plumber."

The ball of popping electricity expanded. Beyond its wavering brilliance, Randy saw the front office in which he'd spent the last twelve years. Twelve years of brooding over his brother's countless successes … twelve years mourning his own failures with nothing but a bottle of cheap liquor to keep him company.

"Go, Randy!" Gingiva said.

He stepped forward. His body tingled as he drew near the magic opening.

"You are a hero," she called after him. "Do what has to be done!"

A swell of dizziness swept over him as he stepped through the rift and fell to the cold tile floor beside his desk. Recovering, he got up and went directly for the back supply room.

There, within a shining steel case, rested the object he sought. Like the great sword of King Arthur, he held the case aloft for a moment, then thrust it into his pocket. From the cabinet Dentin had pried open during his prior visit, Randy grabbed more painkillers and antibiotics.

As he turned back to the shimmering portal, his

heart stuttered at the sight of someone else in the room where Gingiva lay in deep concentration. It was a dark-haired woman, features twisted in a malevolent sneer.

"No!" Randy cried, knowing this must be the witch they'd told him about, the demon's servant freed from the dungeon.

In the blink of an eye, she fell upon Gingiva, and the blue doorway winked out as if it had never been.

"No!" he cried again, hopelessness flooding him.

He paced the office, smashing and kicking everything in his path.

"Motherfucker!!" he cried, tears running down his exhausted face.

An all-too-familiar feeling of failure ate him alive inside. He was born a loser and would die one too. Though he had come to terms with that early on in his miserable life, the thought of Gingiva dying, and the children of Earth being doomed, were unbearable.

Some hero.

He collapsed to the floor and wept.

Dentin looked over his army, the last remaining soldiers in Molarous but for a few hand-picked men he'd left posted to guard the queen.

It wasn't a large crowd, but they burned with the need to avenge those left to rot to death in their beds. They were all equipped with swords of ivory, sharp and gleaming like bolts of lightning in their bearer's hands. Their steel armor and helms bore the insignia of the queen, a single ivory tooth with wings protruding from behind it. Their enameled shields hadn't seen conflict in ages; they shone in the hours between sunset and the rise of the moon.

Even their horses were dressed for war, wearing thick saddle blankets and enameled leather barding. It was hard as stone yet light enough not to over encumber the beasts.

The men rode in silence, their senses keen for any disturbances that would signal an attack. A rutted dirt road led through the forest to the Fang Hill Mountain range, so named for how it appeared to be stone fangs protruding from the earth. There, they would guard the white halls, the hoard of children's teeth.

Dentin kept scanning the horizon, grim with the knowledge that they would more than likely perish defending their most valuable treasure.

The night fell over them and the wind died as they began to ascend into the mountains, heading towards either a calamitous end or the greatest victory the Hyperdontians had ever witnessed.

Gingiva struggled against the grip of the witch's cruel hands at her throat. She'd been unable to hold the rift open, leaving Randy trapped in his own world. Her flesh ached, despite the potency of the pain killing gel he'd applied.

She slapped her attacker away, but Caries viciously grabbed her by the wrists. A small rivulet of blood from the recent extraction still trickled from the tender flesh. Seeing this, and the forceps resting at the edge of the bed, Caries raged.

"Whatever door you thought to open cannot help you now!" She snatched up the stainless steel tool and waved it in Gingiva's frightened face. "I'll wrench every tooth from your body, wretched Wisdom bitch!"

She clamped the forceps onto a pearly white incisor protruding from Gingiva's jaw line and pulled.

The pain was immense; the tooth had rooted itself deep in her jawbone. The witch wiggled and twisted the pliers while Gingiva screamed in agony. There was a crunch and a shot of pain so intense that Gingiva nearly fainted. The witch gritted her own teeth and planted her foot against the side of the bed to use as leverage to yank the healthy tooth from its home. It came out with a spurt of blood as Gingiva wailed.

Caries held it aloft and grinned.

"Just a few hundred more."

She placed her prize in a pocket on the front of her raggedy dress and went in for another.

Gingiva rolled from her bed. She hit the floor hard but didn't have time to let the pain stop her from scrambling to her feet. She pressed her back to the window sill as the witch inched closer. A quick glance over her shoulder made her vision spin from the dizzying heights.

"That's how I got in," Caries said. "Climbed up with my own two hands, using the seams between the teeth as hand and foot holds. Do you see who you are dealing with? I won't stop until I get what I desire, and I desire to yank every one of those pearly whites from your virgin flesh." The witch took another step forward, teasing the Wisdom with such personal knowledge.

"You're vile," Gingiva said, feeling the night wind sweeping over her, stinging the nerves in the empty sockets left from the two teeth she was missing.

"There are no teeth down *there* though; maybe if you survive this someone will give you a good pity brushing."

"Speak for yourself, hag!" Gingiva lunged at the witch before she could push her straight over the windowsill.

They struggled on the floor, raking their nails into each other's eyes. Caries tangled a hand in Gingiva's hair and jabbed the forceps into her toothy cheek. Gingiva screamed as teeth and tender gum tissue were damaged. Caries pulled a second tooth free and palmed it triumphantly.

The door flung open to admit Dr. Maxillary, whose eyes grew wide at the scene.

"Guards!" he cried, perhaps by reflex, forgetting the army had marched. He ran towards the lunatic witch and kicked her in the forehead. His boot was heavy and the strength of his thick leg knocked her away from Gingiva.

Caries sprawled against the wall below the window as Maxillary helped Gingiva to her feet. They were retreating for the open door when her mocking voice halted them.

"I only needed a few anyway," Caries said, having pushed herself up to sit at the window's ledge. "The rest,

I wanted to pry free for pleasure alone."

She flipped backwards and fell into the windswept night. The doctor and Gingiva rushed to the window and looked down to see Caries descending the craggy side of the castle like a spider, making her way in a feverish race toward the dark streets of Molarous and her freedom beyond the gates of the city.

"We must warn Dentin!" Maxillary said. "We must do something!"

But Gingiva already was doing something, lifting a finger to trace the sacred symbol in the air. A tooth dangled loose from its nerves, the aftermath of the witch's final attack. She reached for it, steeling herself against the pain, as she beseeched the old gods to open the portal again.

Randy couldn't remember the last time he'd felt so worthless, so utterly helpless, in all his life.

He went to his desk and yanked the drawer open. His booze stash was empty. He thought about hooking himself up with the laughing gas; maybe this time he could pray to be interrupted by the Hyperdontians.

In a span of only a few hours, he had come to feel like there really was a place for him in life, that he might not be useless at all. But now, here he was, back where he started and more useless than ever.

The sound of a key turning in the lock at the front door caused him to jump; he had no idea why his brother would be creeping into the office so late at night.

He heard muffled voices as he flattened himself against the cabinet behind his desk. It was definitely his brother, Jerry, and a feminine voice. Both slurred and whined with alcohol consumption.

"I love the way you jiggle those things."

"Maybe if you're a good boy I'll take these tassels off."

The reply was like a cold fist n the pit of Randy's stomach.

Tanya. A woman he'd held no delusions of ever being real with, yet it still made him sick to think that his brother had Sherrie at home and still went after Randy's spank material.

"What about your wifey?" Tanya giggled.

"Don't worry about her; she's probably at home fixing me a sandwich for lunch tomorrow."

They both laughed, high and barking laughter that drove Randy to his feet. He glared at them as Jerry sat in one of the front office patient waiting room chairs.

"Then how about a private show?" Tanya was busy removing her bikini top, letting her tits hang in Jerry's face while he made himself comfortable, which apparently involved undoing his pants in preparation.

But Jerry had already spotted Randy.

"What the fuck are you doing here?"

"You left me with a mountain of paperwork, remember?"

"That was hours ago!" Jerry said.

"Well, how the hell would you know how long it would take?" Randy asked. "You've never had to do it yourself."

"That's nice coming from my shit stain brother who never does anything for himself; you wouldn't even have a job if it wasn't for me!"

"Fuck you, Jerry."

"Fuck me?"

"Yeah, fuck you!"

"Well how about you're fired!" Jerry raged.

"Whatever."

"You'll think that when you can't even get a job at the burger barn, loser!"

"Don't call me that!" Randy said, stepping forward.

"Or what?"

Randy fell silent. He had no idea what he would actually do. He was stuck back in a life he didn't really feel like living. Gingiva was probably dead already. All of them were going to die, and it was all his fault.

"You have always been a piece of shit and that will never change," Jerry continued, emboldened by Randy's silence. "Dad always said you'd end up some bum under a bridge, and I believe him."

"Don't you say another fucking word."

"There you go again, being a tough guy. What, did you finally grow a pair of nuts down there?"

Tanya remained quiet, her face twisted into a smile. It was obvious she was struggling not to laugh right in Randy's face.

"What are you smirking at, you filthy whore?" Randy asked.

Her mouth fell open. He could almost see her brain calculating, through a haze of cheap whisky, how she would reply.

"Whatever, you fat piece of crap."

Her words came out, and, surprisingly to Randy, they meant nothing to him. After a lifetime of being concerned with how everyone viewed him, he no longer gave a rat fuck.

Jerry started to speak, but fell silent as a sudden blue light blazed in the hallway.

Randy nearly wept with joy. He grabbed the bag of supplies and readied himself to leave the hell known to him as Earth forever.

Calmly, he turned and looked at his brother, hiding behind the stripper from Peckers.

"Go fuck yourself, Jerry. Take your job and shitty treatment and shove them up your ass."

With that, he passed into the ball of blue lightning that had grown into a doorway.

Into Battle

Randy stumbled in the transition between worlds, nearly falling to his knees beside Gingiva's bed. Joy burst in him to see her alive. Her face bled and there was a gouge between the teeth covering her cheek. But the witch was gone, and she was alive. Doctor Maxillary stood with her, and was quick to assure Randy that Gingiva, although injured, was all right.

"Did you get it?" Gingiva whispered. "Did you get the weapon?"

He lifted the shining case up to the candle light proudly.

"I have to find Dentin and the nameless one. I'm going to put an end to this nightmare."

Just then, a slender figure entered the room. The doctor glanced up and shook his head. "I told you to stay in bed."

"This is not the hour to scold me, Doctor," replied the queen.

She wore resplendent armor that fit her delicate stature perfectly. "I feel my power returning and I wish to fight for my people."

"I retrieved a tool from my world," Randy told her. "I'd like to test it on you first, but I believe it will be a death blow to the demon."

"Come along then and make it fast. Whether I am healed or not, I will go to battle."

"Yes, Your Majesty." Randy glanced down at Gingiva. "Stay here. Doctor Max will watch over you."

She nodded, but as he went to leave her hand caught his. She squeezed it gently, gazing up at him.

"I believe the lady wants a kiss," Bicuspa said.

Randy leaned over and let his lips fall softly against hers. His heart fluttered in his chest. It sent a surge of confidence through him like he'd never felt in his life.

Her trembling, tooth-studded arms gently embraced him, and her voice was soft and sweet in his ear. "Come back ... and come back with the demon's head."

Dentin and his men trod the rough pathway to the chamber of teeth, their horses left behind when the road had become impassable for them.

The kingdom had always kept the treasure in the remote Fang Hill mountain range, hidden away from all who wished to pilfer the enormous hoard.

Dentin moved with all haste, knowing in his heart it was a race between him and the demon. He was a hearty man, a soldier his whole life through, but ascending the mountain side in such a hurry made his legs ache and his lungs burn. He glanced back over his shoulder once the entryway came into sight. His men came along behind him obediently, their faces set in grim expressions of bloodlust.

A rumble beneath his feet shook not only his footing but his determination. A resounding boom echoed between the crags of the Fang Hill range. He turned to see the ancient stone doorway blown to pieces and black smoke roiling from the mouth of the cavern which held the teeth of the Earth children. The men went to their knees as chunks of rubble came down on them like stone shrapnel.

With the smell of smoke was carried the distinct odor of rot, sickening them and igniting a rage in their hearts.

"Forward!" Dentin shouted. "For Molarous, and Queen Bicuspa!"

The army rose and headed onward to battle as the goblins of disease erupted from the cave mouth in an oily, black flood. It was as if the mountain was purging itself of a sickness, vomiting up foes in droves.

Dentin charged, his sword ready to taste the foul flesh of his enemies. His body worked on muscle memory, his mind focused solely on reaching the door, as he cut the tooth trolls into pieces. The stink of them was so foul it made him wonder about their master, how he needed to smell the demon's lifeblood as well. His blade caught a troll as it leapt at him, skewering it. He stared into its eyes, like pustules filled with hatred, as it died. He kicked the corpse free of his sword and continued forward.

His men fought valiantly, a few falling under the rush of attackers, but at last they made it to the doorway. Dentin grabbed a torch from the wall; its illumination fell on a pair of guardians who watched over the queen's treasure. They'd both had their throats torn out; the bite marks of the trolls left such disease that the flesh had already turned septic before their eyes clouded over with death. Dentin knew they couldn't have been dead for more than mere moments.

He proceeded down the winding tunnel, torch in one hand and his sword in the other. It reeked, tarnishing this once sacred place. He had visited it on many occasions with Bicuspa and it had always held the scent of innocence, the feeling in the air that of constant hope and limitless dreams. It was sullied now, perverted by the presence of the tooth demon and his creed.

A hole in the cavern wall showed him where the trolls had tunneled through, and his anger rose. The hoard was close but the enemy had made it there first.

He readied himself. Though he knew his men were right behind him, he felt as if the burden of slaying the beast within the sacred chamber rested solely on his shoulders. His determination multiplied when the memory of the queen's fever-ravished face filled his mind. He strode forward to face the plague bringer, and cut the foul head from his shoulders.

Hammaspeikko heard the commotion of his children

engaging the small army of Hyperdontians. Closing his eyes, he sought the witch. He could feel her heart beating with triumph and he grinned. She was on her way up the mountain, and with her she carried the teeth of a Wisdom.

The time drew nigh. The doorway to the human realm would soon be forced open again. He couldn't wait to taste the fear of the people, to rape their world with his evil. He sat upon the edge of the Hyperdontian treasure, making a throne for himself, the usurper of Molarous… and Earth. He ran his filthy hands through millions of tiny teeth. His touch caused them to decay almost instantly; it filled his wicked heart with a giddiness he hadn't felt in ages.

An armed and armored man entered the torch-lit hall.

"Stand and fight, demon."

"The name is Hammaspeikko," he said, turning to face this upstart. "But you may call me master!"

At the first full view of him, the Hyperdontian faltered. Clearly, what recollections of the plague-bringer's hideousness he'd been told by the dying couldn't hold a candle to his grotesquery in person. Hammaspeikko reveled in being absolute filth, walking pestilence and disease in the flesh.

"I will do no such thing," the man said, regaining his courage. "I will do nothing else but sever your head."

Hammaspeikko rose from his throne, tattered rags flapping around lesion-pocked skin, the smell of decay multiplying when he laughed at the knight's threat. He lifted a handful of baby teeth and let them fall between his fingers; they turned black before they reached the cave floor.

The man did not seem swayed by the show of power; he stood proudly, ready to fight to the death.

"Have it your way, brave fool," Hammaspeikko said. "Allow me to demonstrate to you my true power."

Rearing his head back and gaping his jaws, he inhaled deeply., then unleashed a black blast of fire from his throat.

The knight leapt to the side, crashing through and rolling over piles of teeth as the putrid flame blew past. Although it had no heat, it carried the stench of a thousand unearthed rotting corpses and would steal the breath from his lungs as surely as it ate through his armor. Shielding his face in his hands, the man screamed.

From further down the tunnel came answering screams as the roiling gout of fiery disease and corruption reached the rest of the army. Their torment did not fade with the dying of the fire; it continued as a fever burning through them, bringing crimson hazes of blood to their eyes.

Another figure entered the cavern, casting a disdainful glance at the knight.

"Master," said Caries. "I return, having done your bidding."

Randy followed the queen out onto a wide balcony, where she went directly to the rail and stood with her eyes searching the landscape beyond.

He began to take the laser out of its case but she

halted him with the grip of her small hand.

"I have to try this on you. I'm confident it will kill any infection left," he said.

"The witch has stolen a horse. She has just passed the city gates. We have no time for experiments."

Randy stared out into the darkness below but couldn't see what the queen obviously saw with her magical vision.

"How will we ever catch up to her?"

Bicuspa turned and grasped him by the shoulders. "The wings aren't for show, Mr. Plumber."

He couldn't help but scream as she took flight out over the balcony and dragged him along with her. The sudden drop forced his balls into his throat at the loss of gravity. He clung to the case of the handheld laser for dear life as she corrected their flight path. Her wings beat frantically, keeping them well above the city.

As they passed over it, Randy looked down onto the rooftops of the sleeping citizens. He wondered if their nightmares were about to come true or if he and the queen's army would come out victorious over the plague bringer.

Her grip tightened as they flew over the fortified walls of the city and out over the fields.

"You're so fast!" he cried.

"This is nothing," she answered. "You should see me dart around entire countries."

He saw the small village houses, where Gingiva grew up thinking she was a freak for having flawless skin. The forest approached, causing Bicuspa to fly upward to avoid the treetops. Randy hoped her strength held out or he would end up impaled upon the dry toothy trees below them.

They landed on the side of a mountain that rose into the sky like a giant incisor. She planted him on a rough path before gracefully landing. She was breathing heavily and sweat beaded on her brow before running between the teeth in her flesh. She wobbled on her feet and Randy held her arm to steady her.

"The witch is still ahead of us," she said. "We must stop her."

"You're burning up."

"I have no time for sickness. Come, let us finish this."

They ascended into the highest points of the Fang Hill Mountains. His joints ached, his lungs struggling to get enough oxygen, but he pushed himself to keep up with the Tooth Fairy. A sword hung upon her hip, her armor shone brightly beneath the moon, and her bravery gave him strength.

He had never been courageous in his life, he was a fuck up and had grown to accept it. But that was in another world, he reminded himself. He couldn't let Gingiva down after the sacrifices she'd made. He held the steel case, his weapon for war awaiting to burn into the disease riddled flesh of the tooth demon.

Bicuspa drew her sword and announced, "She has entered the sacred chamber!"

A Sting of a Wasp

Torchlight glittered over a mountainside strewn with the dead and dying. A battle was still taking place, a brave handful of Hyperdontians fighting to the last against a horde of tooth goblins.

The enemy far outnumbered the brave tooth knights, and Randy knew the aftermath would be horrific. The smell, pungent and familiar, told him many of the trolls had perished, but to his dismay and that of the queen, there were far more casualties among her people.

Bicuspa slowed her pace for only a moment, just long enough to look into the face of a fallen soldier. She cursed under her breath and headed onward with a rage clearly displayed in her stride and the way she held her weapon at the ready.

She was a leader and a warrior, ready to avenge every one of her subjects who became victim to the horrors wrought by the one the trolls called Hammaspeikko. Rather than trudging through blood and corpses, she took flight like a humanoid honey bee and buzzed over them straight for the mouth of the cave.

Caries presented the Wisdom's teeth to the demon, who grinned beneath his filthy beard and told her, "You shall be rewarded handsomely."

She smiled and made her way to a mound of baby teeth, scooping up a handful. "Shall I open the doorway now, master?"

"I'm ready," he said. "Prepare to begin your reign as queen."

Caries smiled outwardly but in her heart she still wished her lover could have shared in her glory. She raised her hands, one in a tight fist clenching the still-bloodied teeth torn from Gingiva's flesh and a mixture of baby teeth.

"I call to the old ones, the gods between worlds. I bid you open the doorway to the Earth realm."

An unearthly wind blew back her hair as the chamber filled with bone chilling cold. A voice spoke, hollow and commanding. "You are not a Wisdom."

"I have brought you her teeth, still stained with her blood," Caries replied. "And an offering of children's teeth, innocent and pure."

There was silence.

Trying not to show any anxiety in front of Hammaspeikko, she spoke again. "Open the rift!"

***

Dentin laboriously pushed himself up onto his hands and knees; his body was failing him as the sickness within him ate at his insides. Finding his sword among the scorched hills of teeth, he crept forward as the witch beseeched the elder gods.

She and her demon lord had their backs to him. He saw his chance and took it, rising to plant his blade between her shoulder blades.

The ivory point burst out through her chest, stealing the breath form her lungs before she could scream.

But as she fell, he saw a glowing orb on the other side of her. Even as she crumpled, she threw her sacrifice into it, the void swallowing the teeth hungrily.

Winds blasted Dentin backwards. The old gods were appeased and the portal began to open.

The tooth demon stepped over the dying witch, his eyes wide as he approached the doorway that would birth him into the human world. "Hold it open," he snarled to her. "Hold it open until your last breath!"

Dentin felt flooded with utter failure. The children of earth would become monsters and the legacy of the Tooth Fairy and her people would die and become nothing more than fantasy.

As if sensing his dismay, Hammaspeikko paused to taunt him. "You fool, there is no stopping me. Once Earth is in shambles, I think I shall return here to see what is left of your feeble kingdom"

Dentin forced his fevered body to stand once more. Though his extremities were growing black and gangrenous, he dislodged his sword from Caries' ribs and staggered forward. "Not while I live."

Hammaspeikko laughed uproariously. "As you will, then!" Gaping wide his maw of disease, he prepared to unleash another spray of black fire to consume the nuisance once and for all.

A flash of silver blurred passed Dentin, who had solemnly accepted his imminent death. The shining object hurtled into the abdomen of the demon before he could exhale his poison. Hammaspeikko was knocked sprawling, the windy edges of the rift tugging at his wild hair and beard.

Astride his filthy chest was Queen Bicuspa, sword poised to deal the killing blow.

But before she could, the plague bringer slammed his gnarled fist into her nose. She tumbled away, dazed. His bellow of triumph shook the cavern, bringing the last of his troll-children rushing to him, screaming with bloodlust.

Randy found himself swept up in a rush of bodies, the exhausted remnants of the Hyperdontian army pursuing the retreating trolls. The deadly creatures flooded down the passageway, mouths full of infection, hearts brimming with hatred, answering their master's call. The soldiers followed, trying to cut them in two.

He managed to evade the tumult long enough to don a paper mask and pop the silver case open. The Laser Light 2000 was smaller than he'd thought it would be, a wand of stainless steel with a thin head made for precision. Its handle was smooth and black, its power switch just beneath his thumb.

This was a new tool to him; in his time at dental school, the technology hadn't been so advanced. It ran off of a chargeable battery and held the power to destroy NUGS and trench mouth in a matter of seconds. He turned it on and watched the tip glow blue as the laser indicated it was ready for use.

Shrieks echoed all around him. The stench was thick, the corpses of Dentin's men reminding him of the fate he might face. He held the laser out before him like a miniature sword, pulse racing with utter terror.

Out of the shadows, trolls came at him like a wave of rotten teeth. He lifted his laser, praying it would work; his mind for a second pictured it proving harmless as they tore him to pieces of useless meat.

"Get back you fuckin' Nugs!" he screamed.

The blue glow of the laser head was only a pinprick, but when he stepped into the fray and dashed it across the first wave of oncoming trolls, it cut through them with the ease of Dentin's white blade. They fell back, screaming, their living-disease flesh charred by bright blue fire. Smoking chunks dropped from their limbs. Those struck in the torso collapsed in melting, smoldering pieces to the damp cavern floor.

Randy spun and lunged, stabbing at them mercilessly, shouting incoherent threats and curses.

Those of the second wave, close on their heels, suddenly didn't feel so brave or loyal to their master anymore, not in the face of this wand of blue death. Their charge became a panicked rout, tumbling and trampling over each other as they fled down the tunnel for the freedom of the night.

The way cleared before him, Randy entered the torchlit white chamber, the resting place for billions of baby teeth. His gaze instantly fell on Queen Bicuspa as she fought with the hideous plague bringer. They battled at the edge of an open portal; beyond it was an average American street in the light of the moon, his moon. He knew those families sleeping in that quiet neighborhood would never even realize the nightmare trying to slip into their lives at that very moment.

"Let her be, demon!" he cried. "This is between me and you!"

Bicuspa smiled proudly, blood running from her nose, at the sight of the hero dentist approaching. His mask shielded the bottom of his face, but his eyes burned with a grim fire. He would die in order to prevent the tooth demon from entering the world in which he'd been born.

Hammaspeikko caught her off guard with a swipe of his huge, gangly hand. She was flung backwards, crashing into a hill of baby teeth, the breath knocked from her petite body. One of her iridescent wings broke with a brittle, agonizing snap.

She watched as Randy stomped towards the demon and lifted his weapon, its light minuscule in the great chamber. He came to stand before the beast from the void. Hammaspeikko towered over him, laughing.

"What is that tiny thing? Are you going to write me a letter?"

"Quiet, you bastard!" Randy hollered.

Hammaspeikko swung his fist, but Randy dodged out of its path. He stood shakily, as if remembering his body wasn't made for heroic adventures. Impatient, the demon inhaled, ready to unleash another foul, infectious gale like a dragon spitting fire.

Before he could, the wind from the portal faded to a thin whistle, then sighed to a stillness around them. The witch Caries went limp, the final dregs of life passing from her. Hammaspeikko expended his breath in a howl of frustration.

He spun and darted for the opening as its edges shivered and began to contract .Diving for the closing rift, he jammed his head into it and struggled to force his way through.

His greedy gaze beheld the advanced human civilization. He could smell them, their children sleeping in their beds. A feast, his to plunder, his to ravage and destroy!

A sharp, narrow pain pierced his back, like the prick of a needle, like the sting of a wasp. It spread swiftly through his limbs in a burning so intense that he cried out. His entire body felt caught in a pyre, but he couldn't look back.

His voice echoed among the houses of sleeping humans, the thunderous lamentations of a beast defeated by something no bigger than a dagger. Then, even those echoing cries were defeated, choked off as the portal continued to close. His throat clenched painfully, esophagus crushed by what felt like the force of the universe.

Then his eyes shot from their sockets, and Hammaspeikko saw no more.

Randy watched the blue fire ignite from the wound left by his laser. It burned and ate at the creature made of disease until Hammaspeikko's flesh fell away in charred pieces and his skeleton began to crumble.

The demon's head hung suspended in midair for a few moments more, trapped in the grip of the closing void rift, before being spat back into the realm of the Hyperdontians. It landed on the floor of the sacred chamber, its black blood spreading out in a stinking pool.

He pulled the dental mask from his face and stood over the remains of his foe. Bicuspa came to Randy's side, her broken wing hanging limp. She put her hand on his shoulder and squeezed. On the cavern floor, amidst spills of scorched baby teeth, Dentin stirred and coughed. He sat up and looked down at his body in astonishment; his flesh was returning to its natural hue, abscesses that had already begun to blister and bubble now receding before his white eyes.

"You are a hero, dentist," he said.

Bicuspa nodded. "I can feel my fever has gone."

Randy's lord vampire hypothesis was proven by watching the plague vanish in his companions. He'd killed the demon and its supernatural sickness was dying with it. A group of injured soldiers came into the chamber, their amazement turning to grateful tears.

Dentin moved to stand on his queen's other side, kicking the corpse of the witch on his way.

"Gather it up as a prize of war," he ordered his men, indicating the enormous skull from which Hammaspeikko's flesh had fully rotted.

"What will happen to the children?" Randy asked, gazing at the sullied teeth around him.

"This night may be filled with terrible dreams, " said Bicuspa, "but, luckily for them, those nightmares will never become reality ... thanks to you, Randy Plumber."

Dawn turned the sky into a water-colored dome. A cool breeze blew through the city, crisp and clean. Those at the great gates raised a cry of victory as the heroes on their radiant white horses returned to , sporting the demon's skull on a pike. They bore the trophy proudly as they rode. Flowers were tossed in their path and cheers greeted them, lifting their spirits to a soaring height.

The streets filled with ecstatic citizens, their bodies cured of the invading illness brought by the beast of the void. Already, the walls of the castle beamed white once more. Every tooth adorning it and all of the kingdom of Molarous were healthy and strong. From the top of the steps, Dr. Maxillary waved them onward, his cheeks stained with happy tears.

The procession headed into the main hall of the keep, but Randy ran straight to Gingiva's bedchamber.

He found her waiting by the window, swathed in a soft white dress. Her exposed flesh was pink and healthy, and the teeth armoring her were brilliant in the early morning sunlight.

"We did it!" he cried.

"I watched you ride in," she said. "A hero from a fairytale. We could not have hoped to cast aside this evil without you, Randy."

He gently took her into his arms. Hugging her filled him with a sense of fulfillment.

"What will you do now?" she asked softly.

Randy didn't immediately answer. When he'd first arrived here, he would have happily fled back to his own Earth without a second thought. But, after witnessing the pain, bravery, and nobility of the Hyperdontians ... and after rescuing the beautiful Gingiva ... he found himself confused. The question was like a punch in the gut. Though he'd risked his life to save those people in his world, he wasn't sure he wanted to return...especially after telling Jerry to go fuck himself.

"You can stay here," she whispered. "I know what you're thinking."

He laughed against her golden hair. "Oh, right, I better remember to keep my thoughts pure. I mean, if I'm going to stay."

She drew back to look up into his eyes. "Those other thoughts, I share the same about you."

Randy felt his face redden. Embarrassment silenced him. Gingiva pulled him close again, brought her lips to his, and kissed him softly. It grew more passionate and deep; he could feel himself growing aroused, but was unsure about one aspect of their seemingly budding relationship.

"You do know not every part of my body is studded with teeth, right?" she asked teasingly.

He coughed and stammered, blushing redder than ever.

His body ached when she went on very quietly, looking into his eyes. "I've never been brushed, but who better to do it than a dentist?"

Queen Bicuspa strode briskly down the hall, with Dr. Maxillary following closely behind her.

"Your Majesty," he said, "I do wish you'd sit and let me administer care to that wing."

"Later," she replied. "I must speak with our hero of the day. We'll prepare a great feast in his honor, but I would like to know if I am supposed to be delivering a farewell or a welcome speech."

She pushed open the door to the new Wisdom's room and stopped in her tracks. The doctor peered over her shoulder, eyebrows raising.

"I daresay," he murmured, "that you have your answer."

Randy stood before the queen's pearly throne, clad in

soft leather trousers and a white tunic embroidered with her royal emblem of a winged tooth.

Dentin approached at a slow, ceremonial pace. Balanced across his upraised palms was a brilliant sword. This, with a bow of his head, he offered to the queen. She took it, inclining her head in return.

The crowd packing the great hall held their breaths as she readied to speak.

"We are gathered here to salute you, Randy Plumber," she said. "Your bravery and selflessness saved this entire kingdom, as well as the children of your world. Kneel before me an ordinary man." When he did so, she

touched the tip of the radiant blade to each of his shoulders. "And arise a knight of the realm, head dentist of Molarous, a hero to all Hyperdontians. Our gratitude is unending and our love for you eternal."

Randy couldn't hold back the tears as he stood and received his sword; a new life was just beginning for him. Gingiva beamed at him from the crowd, and his heart filled with joy as the people of the great white city cheered his name.

Jerry Plumber sat dumbfounded in the dark waiting room.

The tassel-titted Tanya had hastily made herself scarce after that craziness with Randy walking into a giant ball of light and vanishing. He didn't blame her. He could hardly make sense of it himself.

He would never forget the way Randy had looked in

the pulsing blue light of some phantom doorway. He'd looked taller, stronger, brave and purposeful, prouder... like a true dentist.

A tear slid down Jerry's cheek.

He wasn't really concerned over losing the relationship he'd had with his brother, or even with how he'd fill Randy's shoes as far as pulling his weight around the practice their father left to them.

No, on dark, lonely nights, he would recall that image and compare himself to it ... and always find himself to be no match for Randy at all.